AF269576

SOFTBALL FUN

by Cari Meister

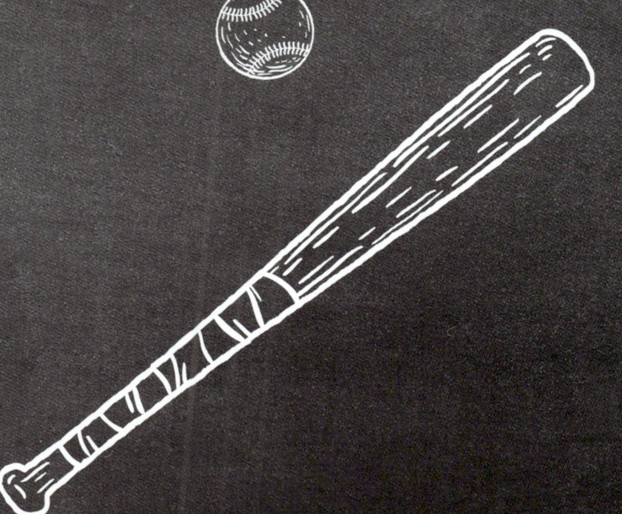

PEBBLE
a capstone imprint

Pebble Emerge is published by Pebble, an imprint of Capstone.
1710 Roe Crest Drive, North Mankato, Minnesota 56003
www.capstonepub.com

Library of Congress Cataloging-in-Publication Data
Names: Meister, Cari, author.
Title: Softball fun / by Cari Meister.
Description: North Mankato : Capstone Press, [2021] | Series: Sports fun | Includes bibliographical references and index. | Audience: Ages 6-8 | Audience: Grades 2-3 | Summary: "Softball is exciting to watch, but it's even more fun to play! Kids can take the field by learning the rules of the sport, the equipment and skills needed to play, and the importance of good sportsmanship. A simple activity helps kids strengthen a basic softball skill"-- Provided by publisher.
Identifiers: LCCN 2020037725 (print) | LCCN 2020037726 (ebook) | ISBN 9781977132291 (hardcover) | ISBN 9781977154910 (pdf) | ISBN 9781977156570 (kindle edition)
Subjects: LCSH: Softball--Juvenile literature.
Classification: LCC GV881.15 .M45 2021 (print) | LCC GV881.15 (ebook) | DDC 796.357/8--dc23
LC record available at https://lccn.loc.gov/2020037725
LC ebook record available at https://lccn.loc.gov/2020037726

Image Credits
Alamy: agefotostock, 5, Steve Skjold, 21, Susan Leggett, 18, Tom Carter, 9, Visions of America, LLC, 16; Getty Images: Comstock Images, 7, Mike Watson Images, 15; iStockphoto: ADonsky, 12, kali9, 6, 19, RBFried, 17, RonTech2000, 13; Shutterstock: Caleb Jones Photo, 11, Rob Marmion, cover, shpakdm, 8, VectorPixelStar, back cover, 1

Editorial Credits
Editor: Jill Kalz; Designer: Tracy McCabe; Media Researcher: Eric Gohl; Production Specialist: Katy LaVigne

All internet sites appearing in back matter were available and accurate when this book was sent to press.

Printed in the United States   5319

TABLE OF CONTENTS

Words in **bold** are in the glossary.

WHAT IS SOFTBALL?

Softball is a fun outdoor sport. It is played with two teams. Each team has nine players. Teams try to hit a ball with a bat. When batters get a hit, they run. They try to touch all the **bases** to score a **run**. The team with the most runs wins.

WHAT DO I NEED?

You need a softball to play softball!
Softballs look like baseballs but bigger.
They weigh more too. Softballs aren't soft.
Softballs are as hard as baseballs.

Each player needs a glove to catch balls.
Most softball players wear a cap. It keeps
the sun out of their eyes.

Softball players need bats. Bats are long and thin. They are made of wood or metal. Batters need to wear a **helmet**. A helmet is hard on the outside. It has soft padding on the inside. A helmet keeps a player's head safe.

WHERE DO I PLAY?

Softball is played on a field. There is an **infield** and an **outfield**. The infield is shaped like a diamond. It is made of sand, clay, or dirt. The outfield is wide and grassy.

The infield has four bases: first base, second base, third base, and home plate. A **mound** is in the middle. A pitcher stands on it to throw the ball to a batter.

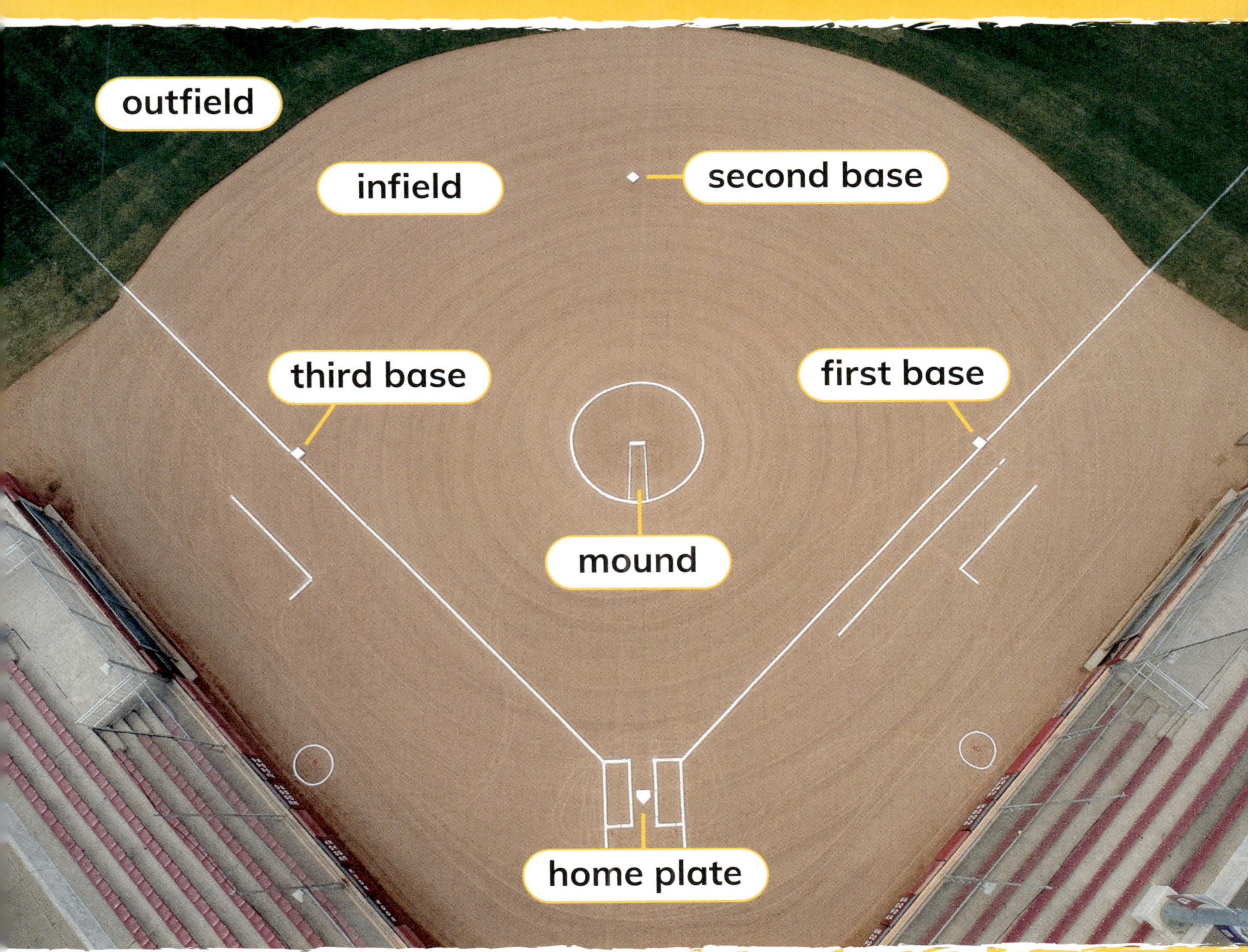

outfield
infield
second base
third base
first base
mound
home plate

HOW DO I PLAY?

A softball game starts with one team at bat. Batters try to hit the ball and score runs. The other team is on the field. They try to keep batters from making runs.

Softball is played in **innings**. A full game is seven innings. Young kids play only five. An inning lasts until the batting team gets three outs. Then the teams switch places.

To bat, a player stands by home plate. The pitcher on the other team throws the ball. The batter tries to hit it. An **umpire** says if the pitch is good or bad.

If the pitch is good, and the batter doesn't swing, it's a strike. If the batter misses the ball, it's a strike too. Three strikes and the batter is out.

Batters run around the bases after hitting the ball. They score a run if they make it back to home plate. The other team tries to stop batters by making outs.

Outs happen when balls are hit in the air and caught. A player may throw a ball to a base before a batter gets there. That is an out too.

HOW CAN I BE A GOOD SPORT?

Being a good sport means playing fair. Learn and follow the rules of the game. Do not cheat. Never argue with an umpire. Listen to your coach.

Being a good sport means being kind.
Work hard. Do your best to learn and get
better. Cheer for your team. Softball is fun
when everyone is a good sport!

SKILL BUILDER: ROCKET RUNNING

Getting off a base quickly is a good skill to have in softball. Try this skill builder. It will help you run the bases faster.

What You Need:

- space to run

- a base or a piece of foam, wood, or cloth that can serve as a base

What You Do:

1. Get in a ready-to-run position. Put one foot on the base. Put your other leg out front, like you are about to take off. Make sure your arms are ready to pump fast.

2. Think of exploding off the base like a rocket. Use
   your back foot to push you off the base.

3. Sprint for about five strides.

4. Return to the base and repeat steps 1 through 4
   five times.

GLOSSARY

base (BAYSS)—a corner of a softball diamond

helmet (HEL-mit)—a hard hat that protects a player's head

infield (IN-feeld)—the inner part of a softball field that includes the bases

inning (IN-ing)—the part of a softball game when players on each team get a turn at bat

mound (MOUND)—a small hill made of dirt, sand, or clay on which a pitcher stands

outfield (OUT-feeld)—the outer, grassy part of a softball field

run (RUN)—a point in softball that's made when a batter touches all the bases

umpire (UM-pyr)—the person who makes sure both teams follow game rules

READ MORE

Bechtel, Mark, and Elizabeth McGarr McCue. *Sports Illustrated Kids Baseball: Then to Wow!* New York: Time Inc. Books, 2016.

Rogers, Amy B. *Girls Play Softball.* New York: PowerKids Press, 2016.

INTERNET SITES

Basic Youth Softball Rules
http://www.kids-sports-activities.com/softball-rules.html

Little League Baseball and Softball
https://www.littleleague.org/

Softball Facts for Kids
https://kids.kiddle.co/Softball